I Don't Want to Wear a Mask

Paul DiPietro

illustrations by
Jennifer Lenox

AUTHORS PLACE
—PRESS—

Published by Authors Place Press
9885 Wyecliff Drive, Suite 200
Highlands Ranch, CO 80126
Authorsplace.com
Copyright 2020 © by Paul DiPietro
Copyright 2020 © Illustrations and Design by Jennifer Lenox
All Rights Reserved

No part of this book may be reproduced or transmitted in any form by any means: graphic, electronic, or mechanical, including photocopying, recording, taping or by any information storage or retrieval system without permission, in writing, from the authors, except for the inclusion of brief quotations in a review, article, book, or academic paper.

The authors and publisher of this book have used their best efforts in preparing this material. The authors and publisher make no representations or warranties with respect to accuracy, applicability, fitness or completeness of the contents of this material. They disclaim any warranties expressed or implied, merchantability, or fitness for any particular purpose. The authors and publisher shall in no event be held liable for any loss or other damages, including but not limited to special, incidental, consequential, or other damages. If you have any questions or concerns, the advice of a competent professional should be sought.

Manufactured in the United States of America.
ISBN: 978-1-62865-797-5

I would like to dedicate this book to my son Evan who brings me joy and happiness every day. His big heart, compassion for others, and thirst for knowledge gives me hope for the future.

Today, Michael and his mother are planning to go to the store to buy groceries.

"Michael," his mother called, "It's time to go. Please get your mask."

Follow up questions:

1. Where are Michael and his mother going?

2. What are some potential concerns with going to a store during COVID-19?

3. What are some things that we can do to protect ourselves when we go to a store?

4. What safety item did Michael's mother ask him to go and get?

Practice Session:

Can you show me some safety equipment that you use when going out into the community?

Michael crossed his arms and stomped his feet. He responded to his mother in a very loud voice,

"I don't want to go and get my mask!

I HATE wearing a mask!"

Follow up questions:

1. How did Michael respond to his mother when she asked him to get his mask?

2. Can you identify the emotion?

3. Why do you think he responded in this way?

4. What could Michael have done differently?

5. How does wearing a mask make you feel?

Michael's mother could see that he was upset, and she suggested that Michael take some deep breaths. So, Michael closed his eyes and, slowly, he breathed,

in and out

in and out

in and out.

Michael began to feel better after taking a few slow, deep breaths.

Follow up questions:

1. Can you identify the coping skills that Michael used when he was upset?

2. What are some coping skills that you use when you are feeling upset?

Practice Session:

Can you demonstrate a coping skill that you use when you are angry?

Once Michael had calmed down, his mother explained why it is important to wear a mask when going out into the community.

"Germs," she said, "can travel from your body to someone else's body if you sneeze, cough or breathe too close to other people. At the store, we will be near lots of other people. If everyone wears a mask, we won't share germs with others. We do not want to get sick, do we?"

Michael thought about this and he shook his head, "no."

"Wearing a mask will help us stay healthy and safe," said his mother.

Follow up questions:

1. What does it mean to be safe? Who or what makes you feel safe?

2. What can you do to be safe while going out into the community during COVID-19?

3. Can you identify how Michael is feeling?

Practice Session:

Can you show me what some different feelings might look like, such as:
Happy, sad, afraid, worried, angry, surprised.

Michael went and found his mask. Finally, he and his mother walked out the door to go to the grocery store.

Follow up questions:

1. What was the problem that Michael had to overcome in this story?

2. How did Michael overcome the problem?

About the Author

Paul DiPietro is a writer and Autism Specialist for the Holyoke MA Public School System. He has been working with individuals with Developmental Disabilities, Autism, and complex behavioral and emotional disabilities for the past 22 years.

Personally, Paul enjoys spending as much time with family and friends as possible, enjoys the ocean, music, cycling, swimming, and traveling. He enjoys sharing his knowledge and experience working with individuals with Autism to build awareness in the community. He believes that through knowledge and education you can inform change within the world.

Paul feels strongly that learning and education is the most important thing for our youth today. He believes in teaching our children not only to be successful but also to improve our world.

Find more about Paul DiPietro at growingupwithcourage.com or growingupwithcourage@gmail.com.

About the Illustrator

Jennifer Lenox is a Vermont artist and illustrator. She runs a custom artwork e-commerce business through Etsy.com, and is a featured artist at several Vermont fine art galleries. This is her first foray into the world of children's book illustration, though she has done technical illustrations for medical and physical therapy publications in the past. Jennifer spent several years teaching art at the elementary and middle level in both Vermont and New York state after earning her bachelors degree in studio art at Nazareth College, in Rochester, NY. Currently, she resides in Vermont with her husband and two young sons. You can find more of Jennifer's work at www.etsy.com/shop/JenniferLenoxVT.

CPSIA information can be obtained
at www.ICGtesting.com
Printed in the USA
LVHW011954101120
671147LV00008B/465